Author biography

Dear readers,Allow me to introduce myself - my name is Ubaida Khan, and I am a writer based in Islamabad, Pakistan, residing in the G-8 sector. Writing is not just a passion for me; it is my way of expressing emotions, ideas, and stories that come to life through the magic of words.Throughout my journey as a writer, I have honed my skills to encompass a diverse range of literary genres. Whether you seek captivating stories that whisk you away to different worlds, heartwarming love tales that touch your soul, thought-provoking poems that resonate with your innermost feelings, or enchanting songs that tug at your heartstrings, I am eager to present my creations to you.Writing has been a source of solace, inspiration, and joy for me. It has granted me the opportunity to connect with countless souls, transcending geographical boundaries and cultural barriers. Each piece I craft is imbued with my genuine dedication and passion, with the sole intention of leaving a lasting impact on those who embark on the journey of my words.I find immense pleasure in exploring the intricacies of human emotions and the essence of life. My writing delves into the various shades of existence, shedding light on the beauty of humanity and the profound experiences that shape our lives.As a writer in Islamabad, I am privileged to be surrounded by the serenity of nature and the rich tapestry of culture that

Pakistan has to offer. These elements often find their way into my works, adding depth and authenticity to my narratives.In this digital age, I am excited to share my literary creations with a global audience, transcending borders and touching hearts across the world. My dedication to the craft drives me to constantly evolve and explore new avenues of storytelling.Thank you for taking the time to acquaint yourself with me and my passion for writing. I look forward to sharing my stories, poems, songs, and more with you in the future. Your support and appreciation mean the world to me, and I am eager to embark on this journey of creativity together.With heartfelt gratitude,Ubaida Khan

Shadows of Enigma A Symphony of Suspense, Thrills, Mysteries, and Horrors

Shadows of Enigma A Symphony of Suspense, Thrills, Mysteries, and Horrors

ubaidakhan

ISBN 978-93-5883-122-1
© ubaidakhan 2023

Published in India 2023 by Pencil

A brand of

One Point Six Technologies Pvt. Ltd.
Unit no. 26, Ground Floor, Building A1,
Wadala Truck Terminal Road,
Near Post Office, Antop Hill, Mumbai - 400037
E connect@thepencilapp.com
W www.thepencilapp.com

DISCLAIMER: *The opinions expressed in this book are those of the authors and do not purport to reflect the views of the Publisher.*

CONTENTS

Title Secrets of the Enchanted Manor

Once nestled deep within the forest, the Enchanted Manor stood tall, its dark silhouette giving off an eerie vibe that kept most villagers at a distance. Rumors of haunting and ghostly apparitions spread like wildfire, scaring away all but the bravest souls. Among those intrigued by the mystery of the manor was a young and curious journalist named Emily.Emily was an adventurous spirit who couldn't resist a good mystery. She'd heard tales of a hidden treasure buried within the manor's walls, and her journalistic instincts drove her to uncover the truth. Armed with her camera, notepad, and a keen determination, she set out to explore the legendary Enchanted Manor.As Emily ventured deeper into the heart of the forest, the atmosphere grew thicker with suspense. Twisted branches reached out like gnarled fingers, and shadows danced beneath the moonlight. Soon, she reached the imposing entrance of the manor. The wooden door creaked open, inviting her in with a haunting whisper.Inside, Emily discovered a world frozen in time. Dust-covered furniture adorned the elegant rooms, and cobwebs hung from every corner. The air was heavy with a mixture of decay and forgotten memories. Emily couldn't shake the feeling that she was being watched.As she delved further into the manor's secrets, she encountered peculiar occurrences.

Doors slammed shut on their own, chilling drafts brushed past her, and disembodied whispers echoed through the halls. Yet, Emily refused to let fear overtake her quest for the truth.In her search for the hidden treasure, Emily stumbled upon an old diary belonging to a former resident of the manor, Sir Edwin Sinclair. The diary spoke of a powerful artifact, rumored to grant its possessor immortality. The artifact had been hidden within the manor, guarded by mystical forces that ensured only the pure of heart could claim it.Emily realized that the treasure she sought was more than just a pile of riches; it held the key to understanding the manor's mysterious past and the events that led to its current state. Determined to unlock the secrets, she studied every word in the diary, slowly unraveling the tragic tale of Sir Edwin and his ill-fated pursuit of immortality.As Emily pieced together the clues from the diary, she started to notice strange symbols etched into the walls of the manor. They appeared to be protective wards, created to keep something or someone contained. It became evident that Sir Edwin's obsession with immortality had unleashed dark forces that were now trapped within the Enchanted Manor.Driven by her journalistic instincts and her newfound understanding of the manor's history, Emily continued her exploration. Along the way, she encountered mysterious figures who seemed to be both ethereal and corporeal. Some were benevolent, pointing her in the right direction, while others tried to lead her astray.During her quest, Emily also befriended a local historian, Professor Jameson, who had studied the manor's history for years. Together, they unearthed more about the dark rituals Sir Edwin had performed in his pursuit of immortality and the consequences it had brought upon the manor and its inhabitants.The more Emily discovered, the more dangerous her journey became. Malevolent spirits began to manifest with increasing frequency, and the line between reality and illusion blurred. Yet, Emily's determination to find the truth pushed her forward.Finally, in the heart of the manor, Emily and Professor Jameson discovered the hidden chamber where the artifact lay. However, as they approached, the sinister forces that had been trapped for so long sensed their presence and awakened. The manor came alive with malevolence, its walls seemingly breathing with ancient maleficence.In a climactic battle of wills, Emily and Professor Jameson faced the wrath of the dark spirits. Drawing strength from their friendship and their pursuit of knowledge, they managed to withstand the onslaught and reach the artifact.But the artifact was not what they expected. Instead of a source of power, it turned out to be a vessel of containment for the malevolent spirits, bound by Sir Edwin's sacrifice to protect the world from their terror.In a moment of selflessness, Emily and Professor Jameson decided to keep the artifact hidden within the manor. They believed that its power should remain contained, lest it fall into the wrong hands and unleash chaos upon the world.And so, Emily returned to her journalistic career, keeping the secrets of the Enchanted Manor close to her heart. The mysteries she unraveled taught her that some secrets are best left untouched, and that the pursuit of truth must always be tempered with responsibility.The Enchanted Manor continued to stand as a testament to the past, reminding all who dared venture near of the dangers of obsession and the importance of cherishing the present. Its secrets remained guarded, waiting for the day when someone else, driven by curiosity and bravery, would once again step through its doors and embark on their own journey of discovery.

Title The Enigma of Haunted Hills

In the heart of rural Pakistan, hidden amidst mist-laden hills, lay an ancient mansion known as Haunted Hills Manor. The locals avoided it like the plague, believing it to be cursed by the restless spirits of its tragic past. Stories of apparitions, eerie sounds, and chilling encounters passed down through generations only fueled the mansion's dark reputation.Amidst the fear and mystery, four friends found themselves drawn to Haunted Hills Manor, intrigued by the chilling tales that surrounded it. Ali, a fearless journalist with a thirst for the truth, saw an opportunity to debunk the myths and superstitions surrounding the mansion. Farah, a passionate photographer, sought to capture the essence of the haunting on film, hoping to find evidence of the supernatural. They were joined by siblings Ayesha and Imran, the former a skeptic, and the latter a believer in the existence of the paranormal.One moonlit night, the friends set out on an adventure to uncover the secrets of Haunted Hills Manor. Armed with cameras, flashlights, and a mix of excitement and trepidation, they made their way to the imposing mansion.As they approached the gates, a chilling wind seemed to whisper through the trees, warning them to turn back. But curiosity and a desire for the truth propelled them forward, their footsteps echoing in the eerie silence.Inside the mansion, the air felt heavy, laden with the weight of forgotten memories. The friends explored its dimly lit corridors, each step resonating with a sense of foreboding. Farah's camera flashed intermittently, capturing fleeting shadows that seemed to dance and dissipate in the corners of the frame.The haunting intensified as they delved deeper into the manor. Doors creaked open on their own, and faint whispers echoed through the halls. Imran's belief in the supernatural grew stronger, while Ayesha clung to skepticism, attributing the phenomena to mere coincidence and imagination.In the mansion's grand library, they stumbled upon a collection of old journals. Written by the mansion's former owner, Sir Haroon Shah, the journals spoke of his obsession with dark arts and the occult. It seemed that he had dabbled in forbidden rituals, hoping to unlock the secrets of the spirit world.As they read, Ali couldn't help but notice a recurring name mentioned in the journals – Mariam, a mysterious woman who seemed to be both a confidante and a muse to Sir Haroon Shah. Her presence was shrouded in enigma, her identity a puzzle waiting to be solved.As they continued their exploration, the haunting intensified, and the friends found themselves feeling increasingly uneasy. Objects moved on their own, and they heard disembodied laughter that sent shivers down their spines. Farah's photographs revealed unsettling images of spectral figures lurking in the shadows.In a moment of quiet reflection, Ayesha shared an unsettling story she had heard from her grandmother. According to the tale, Mariam had been a gifted mystic, possessing the ability to communicate with the spirit world. Sir Haroon Shah, driven by his obsession, sought her guidance in his pursuit of power and immortality.Mariam, fearing the consequences of dark arts, had tried to dissuade Sir Haroon, warning him of the malevolent spirits he might awaken. But his thirst for power knew no bounds, and he had ignored her warnings, leading to a tragedy that left the mansion cursed.Determined to find answers, the friends decided to conduct a séance, hoping to communicate with the spirits that haunted the mansion. In the eerie glow of candlelight, they held hands, their breaths held in anticipation.As the séance began, the atmosphere grew charged with a palpable energy. Ayesha, a natural medium, felt a presence trying to communicate. Faint whispers filled the room, and a sense of sadness and loss hung in the air.Suddenly, the atmosphere changed. The room grew frigid, and a dark force seemed to envelope them. Fear gripped their hearts as an otherworldly voice spoke through Ayesha, revealing the truth of the mansion's curse.The malevolent spirit of Sir Haroon Shah himself had taken hold of the séance, seeking to exact vengeance on those who dared to intrude on his domain. Mariam's spirit, trapped between the realms, pleaded for peace, but Sir Haroon's rage and bitterness overwhelmed her cries.In a desperate bid to break the malevolent spirit's hold, the friends channeled all their energy and empathy into the séance. Ali's determination to expose the truth, Farah's artistic sensitivity, Ayesha's innate connection to the spirit world, and Imran's unwavering belief in the power of goodness combined to form a powerful force.With a burst of collective energy, the friends managed to shatter the malevolent spirit's hold. Mariam's spirit emerged, her ethereal presence radiating with gratitude and peace.As dawn broke on the horizon, the friends emerged from Haunted Hills Manor, their hearts heavy with the weight of their chilling encounter. The mansion still stood, a silent witness to the past, but they had succeeded in bringing peace to its tormented spirits.From that day on, the tale of Haunted Hills Manor took on a new dimension – one of compassion, bravery, and the power of friendship to overcome darkness. The friends' bond had grown stronger through their harrowing experience, and they vowed to cherish the memory of that night forever.Haunted Hills Manor remained an enigma, its secrets guarded by the spirits of the past. But for Ali, Farah, Ayesha, and Imran, it was a story that transcended superstition and folklore. It was a testament to the inexplicable forces that exist in the world, and a reminder that some mysteries are meant to remain unsolved. As they returned to their lives, they knew that the memory of Haunted Hills Manor would forever be etched in their hearts, a chilling reminder of the enigma that haunted the hills.

Title Veil of the Forbidden Shrine

In the heart of a remote village in Pakistan, nestled amid ancient mountains and dense forests, lay an enigmatic shrine shrouded in mystery—the Forbidden Shrine of Kalisar. Its walls were adorned with cryptic symbols and eerie carvings, and locals whispered that it held the power to bestow great blessings or unleash unspeakable horrors.Among the villagers were four friends: Ali, a courageous and curious young man; Ayesha, an inquisitive historian with a passion for the supernatural; Fahad, a skeptical and rational-minded engineer; and Zara, a gifted clairvoyant whose visions often unnerved her.One fateful evening, as the sun dipped behind the mountains, the friends found themselves discussing the legends surrounding the Forbidden Shrine. Ayesha had stumbled upon ancient texts that hinted at its existence, and she was eager to explore the truth behind the myths. Intrigued by her findings, the others agreed to accompany her on the quest for the shrine.Guided by a local elder's cryptic directions, they embarked on a journey into the heart of the wilderness. As they ventured deeper into the forest, a sense of foreboding engulfed them. The trees seemed to whisper warnings, and the wind carried haunting melodies through the leaves.After days of arduous travel, they arrived at the edge of a clearing where the Forbidden

Shrine loomed. It stood as a testament to time, its weathered stones adorned with fading symbols of forgotten civilizations.Unfazed by the eerie atmosphere, Ali led the way into the shrine, followed closely by Ayesha and Fahad. Zara, however, felt a growing sense of unease. Her visions had intensified, warning her of an ancient malevolence that guarded the shrine's secrets.Inside the shrine, they discovered a vast chamber adorned with relics of a bygone era. As Ayesha studied the carvings, Fahad remained skeptical, attributing the eerie atmosphere to mere superstitions.Zara, however, felt a magnetic pull towards a hidden alcove. Her visions guided her, revealing images of ancient rituals and a sense of impending doom. With trepidation, she shared her visions with the others, warning them of the shrine's potential dangers.But curiosity won over caution, and they pressed on. Ali discovered an ancient scroll, written in an obscure language. With Ayesha's help, they deciphered the text, revealing the shrine's history and its connection to an ancient cult that had worshipped malevolent entities.As they delved deeper into the shrine's secrets, Zara's visions grew stronger. She saw glimpses of a malevolent spirit, one that had been bound within the shrine to prevent it from wreaking havoc upon the world. The cult's rituals had served to contain this malevolence, but the passage of time had weakened the bonds, allowing the spirit's power to seep through.As night fell, the shrine seemed to come alive with an ominous energy. Shadows danced on the walls, and chilling whispers echoed through the chamber. Ali's bravado wavered, and even Fahad's skepticism began to falter in the face of the mounting supernatural occurrences.Zara, however, felt compelled to confront the malevolent spirit. Drawing on her psychic abilities, she attempted to communicate with the entity. The spirit's presence overwhelmed her, but she persisted, seeking to understand its torment and offer it solace.In a moment of terrifying revelation, Zara learned the truth—the spirit was once a young girl named Laila, who had been sacrificed by the cult in their pursuit of power. Her innocent soul had been consumed by rage and pain, fueling the malevolence that now haunted the shrine.Moved by Laila's tragic fate, Zara sought to help her find peace. She channeled her empathetic energy, reaching out to Laila's tormented soul. Slowly, the malevolent spirit's fury began to subside, and the shadows in the shrine receded.The friends realized that Laila's vengeful spirit was not inherently evil but a victim of the cult's sinister machinations. Zara's compassion had touched the girl's soul, easing her pain and granting her a semblance of peace.As dawn broke, bathing the shrine in a gentle glow, the friends emerged from the Forbidden Shrine, forever changed by their harrowing encounter. The malevolent entity that had once haunted the shrine was now a tragic spirit seeking redemption.Word of their journey spread through the village, and the Forbidden Shrine became a symbol of hope and caution. The friends vowed to keep its secrets hidden from those who sought to exploit its power, knowing that true wisdom lay in respecting ancient forces beyond human comprehension.The Forbidden Shrine of Kalisar remained a place of mystery, guarded by the spirits of its past. For Ali, Ayesha, Fahad, and Zara, it was a reminder of the interplay between darkness and light, and the transformative power of empathy in the face of horrors beyond imagination. Their bond, forged through the veil of the supernatural, would forever serve as a beacon of courage and compassion in the world of the unknown.

Title The Haunting of Dar-ul-Aman

In the heart of Lahore, Pakistan, stood the imposing Dar-ul-Aman, an ancient mansion with a dark history. For generations, the mansion had been the residence of the influential Rahman family, but now, it lay abandoned and shrouded in eerie silence. Locals spoke of strange occurrences within its walls, and tales of a malevolent presence had spread like wildfire.Among those intrigued by the mansion's mysteries were four intrepid individuals: Zahra, a determined and inquisitive journalist; Hassan, a skeptical but open-minded paranormal investigator; Fatima, a compassionate and empathetic psychologist; and Imran, a fearless and adventurous urban explorer.Drawn by the rumors of the mansion's haunting, they decided to explore the enigmatic Dar-ul-Aman one moonlit night. Armed with flashlights, cameras, and a mix of trepidation and excitement, they stepped through the overgrown garden and approached the grand entrance.As they crossed the threshold, the atmosphere grew heavy with an otherworldly presence. Shadows seemed to dance on the walls, and chilling gusts of wind whispered through the halls. Despite the unnerving ambiance, the friends pressed on, eager to uncover the truth.Inside the mansion, Zahra's journalistic instincts kicked in as she captured the haunting details on camera. Fatima felt a profound sense of sadness, as if the mansion itself held onto the weight of its past. Imran, undeterred by the chilling atmosphere, led the way, exploring every room and hallway.Hassan, ever the skeptic, remained cautious, attributing the unsettling events to natural causes. However, as the night wore on, even he couldn't deny the inexplicable occurrences. Doors creaked open on their own, strange whispers echoed through the halls, and ghostly figures seemed to flit at the edge of their vision.In one room, they discovered old diaries belonging to the Rahman family. As they delved into the pages, they learned of a tragic incident that had befallen the family years ago—an unexplained death that had left the mansion in a state of mourning and unrest.The friends soon realized that the malevolent presence haunting Dar-ul-Aman was linked to the unsolved mystery of the Rahman family. Fatima sensed a strong energy of resentment and anger that permeated the mansion, as if seeking justice for a crime left unpunished.Intrigued by the diaries' revelations, Zahra delved deeper into the family's history. She learned that the death of a young girl named Ayesha had cast a dark shadow over the mansion. Ayesha was rumored to have had psychic abilities, and her mysterious demise had been hushed up by the Rahman family, leaving her restless spirit trapped within the mansion's walls.As the friends ventured further, they encountered an eerie room with a peculiar symbol etched into the floor. Imran recognized it from his research—a symbol associated with ancient rituals and summoning spirits.Their exploration led them to believe that the Rahman family had dabbled in the occult, possibly trying to communicate with Ayesha's spirit. But the rituals had gone awry, leading to unintended consequences and the unleashing of a malevolent force.As the night grew darker, the haunting escalated. Zahra's photographs captured fleeting glimpses of apparitions, and Fatima sensed the spirit's growing malevolence. Hassan's skepticism waned, replaced by a deep sense of unease.In a pivotal moment, Zahra discovered a hidden chamber beneath the mansion. Inside, they found remnants of an abandoned ritual, confirming their suspicions that the Rahman family had sought to communicate with the afterlife.As they explored the chamber, a sudden gust of wind slammed the door shut, trapping them inside. Panic set in, and they realized that the malevolent spirit was unleashing its wrath upon them.In the face of danger, the friends banded together, drawing strength from their camaraderie and determination to uncover the truth. Fatima called upon her training to calm the restless spirit, while Hassan used his knowledge of paranormal investigations to appease the entity.As Zahra held her camera, she noticed that the spirit's presence was growing weaker, as if their collective will to understand and bring peace had an impact. The chamber's oppressive atmosphere began to ease, and the door creaked open, freeing them from its grasp.In a moment of revelation, Zahra uncovered a final diary written by Ayesha herself. The diary told a heartbreaking tale of a young girl misunderstood and feared for her gifts, leading to her accidental death during the family's ill-fated ritual.With newfound empathy, the friends understood that the malevolent presence was the result of Ayesha's lingering pain and confusion. They realized that the spirit sought closure and an end to the torment that had bound her for so long.As dawn broke, bathing the mansion in soft light, the friends made a decision to put the spirit to rest. Fatima and Hassan performed a cleansing ritual, guided by Imran's research on ancient practices. Zahra read aloud Ayesha's final diary entry, offering her the understanding and compassion she had longed for.In that moment, the malevolent presence began to dissipate, and the mansion's haunting energy subsided. The spirit of Ayesha, finally at peace, moved on from Dar-ul-Aman, leaving the mansion to its silence once more.Word of their encounter spread, and Dar-ul-Aman became a cautionary tale in the town. The friends' journey had been an exploration of not only the supernatural but also the human psyche. They had faced their fears, learned the value of empathy, and unraveled the mysteries of a haunted past.For Zahra, Hassan, Fatima, and Imran, the haunting of Dar-ul-Aman would forever be a testament to the transformative power of understanding and compassion in the face of horror. And as they walked away from the mansion, they knew that their bond as friends had grown stronger, connected by the shared experience of the haunted and the haunting.

Title The Enigmatic Obsidian Box

In the bustling city of Karachi, Pakistan, the marketplaces thrived with colors and chatter. Amidst the vibrant chaos, an old antiques shop stood, its shelves laden with artifacts from a bygone era. The shop was owned by Mr. Saleem, an elderly man with an air of mystery about him. Locals whispered that he possessed a collection of rare and peculiar items, each with its own haunting tale.Among the curious souls drawn to the shop were four friends: Ayesha, a brilliant archaeologist with an insatiable hunger for history; Farhan, a tech-savvy enthusiast fascinated by the unknown; Sana, a talented artist with a vivid imagination; and Adnan, a level-headed and skeptical engineer.One day, while browsing the shop's wares, the friends stumbled upon an intriguing obsidian box. It bore intricate carvings of ancient symbols, its smooth surface cool to the touch. Mr. Saleem noticed their interest and revealed that the box had a storied past, dating back to a time of dark rituals and unsolved mysteries.As the friends gazed upon the enigmatic box, Mr. Saleem shared the tale of its origins. Legend had it that centuries ago, a sorcerer named Malik Waseem had crafted the box to harness powerful energies and commune with spirits. But the box's true nature remained an enigma, as the sorcerer vanished without a trace, leaving behind only whispers of his arcane knowledge.Intrigued by the box's history, Ayesha proposed a daring idea—to unravel its secrets through a series of experiments and research. Farhan's enthusiasm was contagious, and Sana was excited at the prospect of capturing the box's enigmatic essence through her art. Adnan, although skeptical, agreed to accompany his friends on their quest.Their journey into the box's mysteries began with meticulous research and deciphering ancient texts. As Ayesha delved into archives and Farhan sifted through digital records, they stumbled upon a passage that hinted at the box's power to grant great wisdom or unleash malevolence.Unfazed by the warnings, the friends were determined to uncover the truth. Ayesha's archaeological expertise led them to an underground chamber, believed to be the resting place of Malik Waseem's lost knowledge. As they entered, a chill ran down their spines, and they felt a weight of ancient energy in the air.In the dimly lit chamber, they found a collection of artifacts, each imbued with its own arcane aura. Among them was a grimoire that contained Malik Waseem's writings. Sana was fascinated by the symbols and inscriptions, recreating them on her canvas with haunting precision.As the friends studied the grimoire, they discovered that the obsidian box was an instrument of balance—a key to accessing both light and darkness. Malik Waseem had believed that its power lay in the intentions of the one who wielded it. With great care and preparation, the box could unlock hidden wisdom and reveal truths beyond comprehension.But the box's malevolent side also had its dangers. If its power fell into the wrong hands or if used recklessly, it could unleash chaos and malevolence, feeding off negative emotions and desires.Their curiosity now tinged with trepidation, the friends made a pact to use the box's power responsibly and with utmost caution. Ayesha devised a plan to conduct a ritual that would connect them to the box's energy while keeping them grounded in reality.As the night of the ritual approached, the friends gathered in the underground chamber. Surrounded by the artifacts and with Sana's mesmerizing paintings as their backdrop, they began the ceremony with a mix of awe and apprehension.With the obsidian box at the center, they chanted ancient incantations and focused their intentions on seeking enlightenment rather than power. Slowly, the box seemed to pulse with energy, responding to their harmonious vibrations.As they connected with the box's power, they experienced visions and insights beyond comprehension. Ayesha saw fragments of lost civilizations, Farhan glimpsed glimpses of advanced technologies, Sana's art came alive with ethereal spirits, and Adnan felt a profound sense of unity with the universe.In their quest for wisdom, they realized that the box's true power was not in controlling the supernatural but in understanding and embracing the mysteries of life. They had become the custodians of ancient knowledge, committed to using it to benefit humanity.But as they were about to conclude the ritual, a sudden surge of malevolence threatened to engulf them. Adnan's skepticism turned to alarm as he realized that their intentions had inadvertently attracted dark energies.With great effort, the friends managed to sever their connection to the malevolent force. The box's energy subsided, and they felt an overwhelming sense of relief. They knew that they had to be vigilant, as the allure of power and knowledge could easily lead to corruption.As they emerged from the underground chamber, the sun began to rise, illuminating the city with a golden hue. The friends realized that their journey with the obsidian box had forever changed them. They had embarked on a thrilling exploration of the unknown, learning that some mysteries were meant to be embraced, not conquered.From that day on, the obsidian box remained a symbol of their friendship and the endless quest for knowledge. The friends kept it safely hidden, knowing that its true power was not in its mysterious energy but in the bond they had forged through their shared experience.The legend of the obsidian box continued to echo through the bustling streets of Karachi, a story of friendship, curiosity, and the fine line between light and darkness. For Ayesha, Farhan, Sana, and Adnan, it was a testament to the transformative power of curiosity and the wisdom to respect the mysteries that lay beyond our understanding.

Title The Enigma of the Whispering Pines

In the remote region of Abbottabad, Pakistan, nestled amidst the dense forest, lay a small village named Naveedabad. The village was home to a chilling legend— the Whispering Pines. Tales spoke of haunted pines that emitted eerie whispers, an unsolved mystery that had perplexed the villagers for generations.Among the curious minds drawn to the enigmatic legend were four childhood friends: Amina, a spirited and adventurous young woman; Rafiq, a level-headed and rational thinker; Sahar, a gifted artist with a deep connection to the spiritual world; and Farid, a stoic and determined individual with a penchant for solving puzzles.As the stories of the Whispering Pines reached their ears, the friends were both intrigued and unnerved. Eager to unravel the truth, they decided to embark on a quest to uncover the secrets behind the haunting legend.With their backpacks filled with essentials, they set off into the heart of the forest. The whispering wind welcomed them as they ventured deeper into the mysterious woods, where sunlight struggled to penetrate the thick canopy of ancient trees.As night fell, the forest seemed to come alive with strange noises, causing shivers to run down their spines. Still, the friends pressed on, determined to face the unknown. Guided by Rafiq's logical approach, they followed the faint whispers that led them to an isolated clearing—a place where the haunting was said to be most profound.In the clearing, they found a group of pine trees with unusually twisted trunks. The wind brushed through the branches, producing an unsettling symphony of whispers that seemed to echo from beyond the grave.As Amina and Rafiq investigated the phenomenon, Sahar sensed a powerful spiritual presence lingering within the forest. Her intuition told her that the haunting was more than just a mere natural occurrence.Farid, too, was intrigued by the puzzle before them. He noticed peculiar markings on the trees and deduced that they might hold the key to unraveling the haunting's enigma. Together, the friends vowed to dig deeper into the forest's secrets.Over the following days, they immersed themselves in research, delving into ancient texts and seeking the wisdom of the village's elder. The elder revealed that the Whispering Pines were believed to be a portal between the realms of the living and the dead, a bridge through which spirits could communicate with the mortal world.Undeterred by the eerie revelations, the friends continued their investigation. Sahar, gifted with her artistic sensibility, sketched intricate drawings of the markings on the trees. Amina and Rafiq cross-referenced their findings with historical records, unearthing stories of a tragic love affair that had taken place in the forest centuries ago.The tale spoke of a forbidden love between two young souls from rival tribes. They had chosen the Whispering Pines as their secret meeting spot, knowing that it was a place where their love could be shared without judgment. However, their love had been discovered, leading to a tragic end, with both souls perishing in the forest.As the friends pieced together the puzzle, they realized that the restless spirits of the ill-fated lovers were trapped within the Whispering Pines, unable to find peace. The haunting whispers were their desperate attempts to reach out to the living, seeking resolution and closure.Empathy filled their hearts, and they vowed to help the spirits find peace. Sahar decided to conduct a spiritual ritual, connecting with the ethereal realm and offering solace to the tormented souls. Her artistic talents became the conduit for her spiritual energy, and she created a mural depicting the tragic love story of the two souls.As the mural took shape, the haunting whispers seemed to soften, as if acknowledging the friends' intentions. A strange luminescence emanated from the Whispering Pines, enveloping the clearing in an ethereal glow.In a moment of profound connection, the spirits of the ill-fated lovers appeared before them, their ethereal forms expressing gratitude for the friends' efforts. Sahar's spiritual ritual had opened a pathway for them to find peace and move on from their tragic past.As the spirits dissipated into the night, the forest fell into a deep silence. The Whispering Pines were no longer haunted by tormented souls, and the eerie whispers became faint echoes of the past.Word of the friends' remarkable feat spread through Naveedabad, and the legend of the Whispering Pines transformed from a chilling tale into a story of compassion and resolution. The village celebrated their bravery and compassion, honoring the friends for their role in ending the haunting that had plagued the Whispering Pines for centuries.For Amina, Rafiq, Sahar, and Farid, the quest had been an extraordinary journey into the realm of the unknown. Their bond had grown stronger, cemented by their shared experiences with the supernatural. The Whispering Pines would forever remain a part of their memories, a reminder of the power of empathy and the unbreakable connection between the living and the dead.

Title The Haunting of Ravenswood Manor

Nestled on the outskirts of a quaint little town, Ravenswood Manor stood tall, its eerie presence casting a dark shadow over the surrounding landscape. Legends of its haunted past had been passed down through generations, warning everyone to stay away from its ominous gates. Among those captivated by the chilling tales was a curious young woman named Amelia.Amelia was an adventurous soul, drawn to mysteries like a moth to a flame. She had an insatiable desire to unravel the unknown and understand the unexplainable. The legends surrounding Ravenswood Manor had piqued her curiosity, and she couldn't resist the urge to explore the foreboding mansion.Ignoring the villagers' pleas and fueled by her determination, Amelia set out one gloomy afternoon, following an overgrown path that led to the mysterious manor. As she approached the wrought-iron gates, a cold shiver ran down her spine, but she pressed on undeterred. With each creak of the gates and crunch of leaves underfoot, the tension in the air grew palpable.Inside the manor, Amelia found herself surrounded by an atmosphere that seemed frozen in time. Dusty portraits adorned the walls, their gazes following her every move. Cobwebs stretched across the ceilings like intricate lace, and the air was thick with an otherworldly presence. Amelia's heart pounded in her chest, but she couldn't turn back now.As she ventured further into Ravenswood Manor, Amelia noticed peculiar signs of the supernatural. Mysterious footsteps echoed in empty corridors, and the faint sound of a haunting melody drifted through the air. Yet, Amelia's courage and thirst for the truth pushed her forward.One night, as the moon hung full and luminous in the sky, Amelia heard a distant cry that sent shivers down her spine. She followed the sound to a hidden passage concealed behind a bookshelf. As she stepped through the narrow corridor, she entered a chamber filled with ancient tomes and mystical artifacts.Among the dusty books, she discovered a leather-bound journal belonging to a former resident named Evangeline Ravenswood. The journal recounted a tale of love and betrayal, of dark rituals and a curse that had befallen the manor centuries ago. The more Amelia read, the clearer it became that the tormented spirits of Ravenswood Manor sought revenge for the sins committed against them.Driven by empathy and a desire to help the restless souls, Amelia embarked on a journey to lift the curse that bound them. Armed with knowledge from the journal, she sought out the assistance of a renowned paranormal investigator named Professor Samuel Blackwood.Professor Blackwood was a skeptic at heart, but his curiosity was piqued by Amelia's story. Together, they delved deeper into the history of the manor, unearthing forgotten secrets and hidden truths. They discovered that the key to breaking the curse lay in reuniting two long-lost lovers whose tragic fate had started the chain of events that led to the haunting.As Amelia and Professor Blackwood worked tirelessly to unravel the mystery, they faced unexplainable phenomena. Objects moved on their own, ghostly apparitions appeared in the corners of their vision, and eerie whispers filled the air. The boundary between the living and the dead blurred, and they found themselves entwined in the haunting web of Ravenswood Manor.In their pursuit, they unearthed the forgotten crypt beneath the manor, where the spirits lay trapped and tormented. Guided by the memories of Evangeline Ravenswood, Amelia and Professor Blackwood performed a ritual to reunite the spirits of the long-lost lovers and offer them closure.In a breathtaking climax, the curse was finally broken, and the restless spirits found peace. The mansion, once filled with sorrow and despair, now seemed to breathe with newfound life and hope.As Amelia and Professor Blackwood bid farewell to Ravenswood Manor, they knew that the haunted mansion would forever hold a place in their hearts. They had learned that sometimes, the most haunting mysteries were not the ones that lurked in the darkness, but the ones that resided within the human heart.From that day on, Ravenswood Manor was no longer a place of dread, but a symbol of triumph over darkness and a testament to the power of love and forgiveness. The story of Amelia and Professor Blackwood's daring adventure spread throughout the town, inspiring others to embrace the unknown and face their fears.And so, Ravenswood Manor stood tall, its dark history transformed into a tale of courage, compassion, and the enduring spirit of humanity. Its doors remained open to those seeking answers and the thrill of the unknown, inviting them to explore the mysteries that lie hidden in the shadows of the past.

Title The Haunting of Blackwood Manor

In the heart of a remote countryside, surrounded by dense forests and mist-shrouded mountains, stood Blackwood Manor, an ancient estate with a dark history. Legend had it that the manor was cursed, haunted by vengeful spirits seeking retribution for a long-forgotten tragedy.The manor's unsettling past dated back to the 19th century when it was owned by the tyrannical Lord Samuel Blackwood. He was infamous for his cruelty towards the villagers who worked on his land, subjecting them to harsh conditions and unfair treatment. The villagers lived in constant fear, their pleas for mercy falling on deaf ears.One fateful night, a group of villagers decided to rebel against Lord Samuel's tyranny. Led by a brave and resourceful woman named Amelia, they gathered outside the manor, demanding justice for their suffering. But their attempt at rebellion was brutally crushed by Lord Samuel and his loyal henchmen.As the villagers lay defeated, Lord Samuel condemned Amelia to a horrifying fate – he locked her in a secret chamber beneath the manor, where she was left to suffer and die in darkness. Her anguished screams echoed through the halls, and her spirit was said to have never found peace.From that day on, Blackwood Manor became a place of dread. Villagers avoided it at all costs, fearing the restless souls trapped within its walls. But as the years passed, the manor's sinister allure only grew stronger, drawing thrill-seekers and paranormal enthusiasts from all over.Among those drawn to the legends of Blackwood Manor were four friends: Alex, the skeptical journalist with a penchant for debunking myths; Emma, the fearless photographer eager to capture the supernatural on film; Ryan, the thrill-seeker always chasing the next adrenaline rush; and Sarah, the sensitive and intuitive member of the group, who believed in the existence of otherworldly forces.Together, the friends decided to venture into Blackwood Manor one fateful night. Armed with cameras, flashlights, and a mix of trepidation and excitement, they braved the creaking gates and stepped into the heart of darkness.The manor seemed to come alive with their presence. Cold drafts whispered through the corridors, and eerie shadows danced on the walls. Emma's camera flashed intermittently, capturing fleeting glimpses of spectral figures. Ryan couldn't help but feel an electric thrill as he explored the decrepit rooms, hoping to encounter something truly horrifying.As the night deepened, the friends noticed strange occurrences: doors opening and closing on their own, phantom footsteps echoing through the halls, and the chilling sensation of being watched. Sarah's unease grew, sensing the presence of something malevolent lurking in the shadows.Their exploration led them to the secret chamber beneath the manor where Amelia had met her tragic end. The air grew thick with sorrow and anguish, and Sarah felt an overwhelming urge to free Amelia's tormented spirit.Venturing deeper into the chamber, they found an ancient key hidden beneath a layer of dust. Unbeknownst to them, this was the very key that had sealed Amelia's fate all those years ago. Ignoring the foreboding aura, Sarah used the key to unlock the chamber's hidden door, revealing a sight that chilled them to their core.Within the chamber, Amelia's ghostly figure materialized before them, her eyes filled with both sorrow and rage. Her anguished cries pierced the silence, causing the friends to recoil in horror. It was clear that her spirit sought retribution, not only for her own suffering but for the countless others who had suffered at Lord Samuel's hands.Fear and guilt washed over the friends as they realized the gravity of the malevolent force they had unleashed. Sarah, desperate to quell Amelia's spirit, reached out with empathy, seeking to understand her pain and offer solace.In a moment of eerie calm, Amelia's figure wavered, as if contemplating Sarah's genuine compassion. The friends held their breath, unsure of what would happen next.Amelia's spirit slowly began to fade, the tortured look in her eyes replaced by a semblance of peace. In that moment, Sarah's connection with the vengeful spirit seemed to have broken the cycle of suffering that had plagued Blackwood Manor for so long.The friends fled the manor, their hearts heavy with the weight of the night's events. As they stepped out into the pale light of dawn, they knew that Blackwood Manor would forever hold the echoes of its dark past. But perhaps, with Amelia's spirit finding some semblance of peace, the manor's curse would finally begin to lift.In the days that followed, the friends decided to keep their encounter with Amelia's spirit a secret, protecting the sanctity of the manor and the newfound peace they had brought to it. They hoped that with time, the legends of Blackwood Manor would fade into mere folklore, and its chilling history would serve as a cautionary tale against the dangers of cruelty and tyranny.And so, the haunting of Blackwood Manor came to an end, but its memory would forever linger in the hearts of the four friends. They had faced the horrors of the supernatural, but more importantly, they had learned the power of empathy and compassion in the face of darkness. It was a lesson they would carry with them for the rest of their lives, a reminder that sometimes, true horror lay not in the unknown, but in the depths of the human heart.